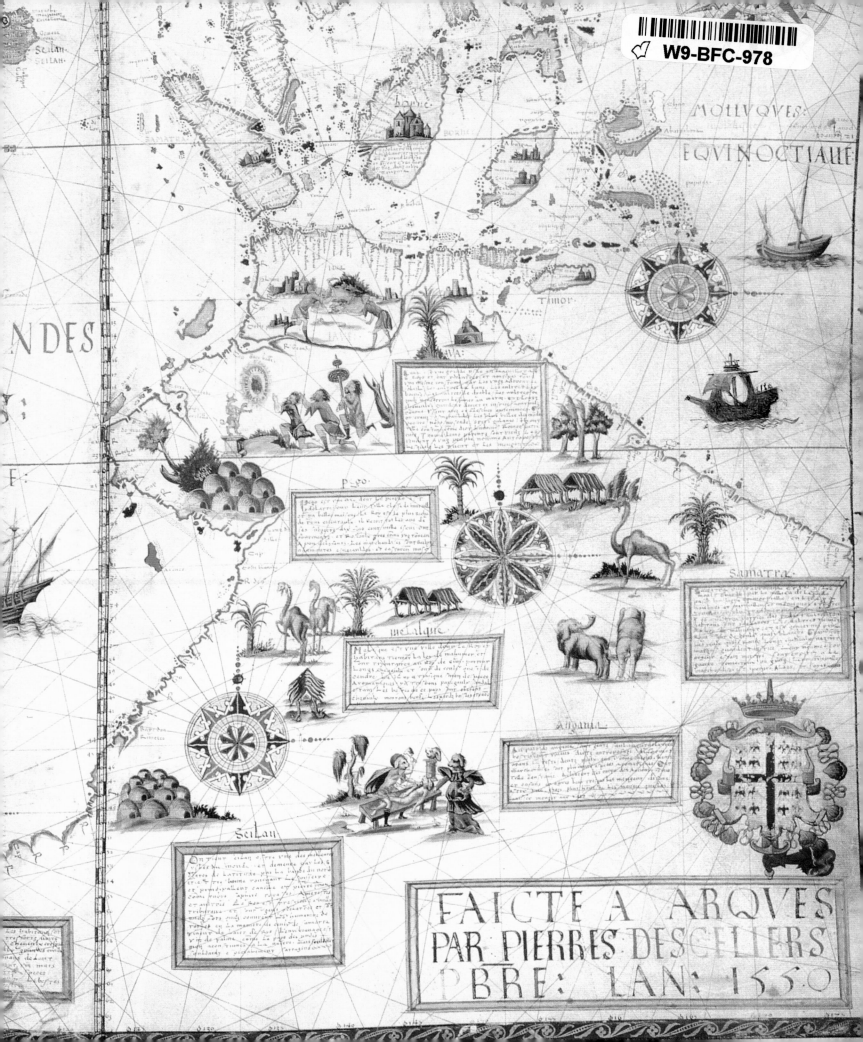

a minedition book
published by Penguin Young Readers Group

Text and illustrations copyright © 2005 by Robert Ingpen
English text edited by Kathryn Bishop
Coproduction with Michael Neugebauer Publishing Ltd., Hong Kong.
Rights arranged with "minedition" Rights and Licensing AG, Zurich, Switzerland.

Published simultaneously in Canada.
Manufactured in Hong Kong by Wide World Ltd.
Designed by Michael Neugebauer
Typesetting in ITC Garamond
Color separation by Fotoreproduzioni Grafiche, Verona, Italy.

Library of Congress Cataloging-in-Publication Data available upon request.

ISBN 0-698-40025-9
10 9 8 7 6 5 4 3 2 1
First Impression

For more information please visit our website: www.minedition.com

THE VOYAGE OF THE POPPYKETTLE

ROBERT INGPEN

minedition

A long time ago a community of tiny fishermen called the Hairy Peruvians lived on a beach near Callao in Peru. Every day they got into their tiny canoes, made from bundles of reeds tied together, and their friend the big Brown Pelican showed them where to catch the anchovy fish of the Pacific Ocean.

Their canoes were so small, and the sea was so big, that they never went out very far. Always in view were the mighty Andes Mountains, home of the Noble Incas.

These Noble Incas were conquered when the Shining Spaniards invaded Peru. The Shining Spaniards were greedy and fierce, and a group of Hairy Peruvians decided they needed to find a new home.

"We will discover what lies beyond the straight line between sea and sky, where the sun sinks every evening," they said. "Perhaps there we will find our new home."

They knew their tiny canoes could not go so far, and so they asked the Brown Pelican for help.

"My friend the Silverado Bird lives high in the mountains," the Brown Pelican said. "He is wise and will be able to tell you what to do. I can carry all seven of you on my back."

So the little band of five men and two women climbed onto the back of the Brown Pelican, and he flew them high into the mountains.

The Brown Pelican found the Silverado Bird who listened carefully to his story about finding a suitable ship for the Hairy Peruvians.

He thought about it and finally said, "I know the answer. Come with me to a special place, to the temple city of Machu Picchu." The Silverado Bird knew the sacred city well; it was on a mountain that rose high into the clouds above the tumbling Urubamba River.

But later, when the Hairy Peruvians looked down on it, from their perch on the Brown Pelican's back, they saw that the city lay in ruins.

The Shining Spaniards had been there. This time they had driven everyone from the city and stolen their treasures. About the only thing that remained were the massive stone walls.

Standing on a shelf by the temple well, however, was an unbroken clay pot. Its unusual shape made it look like some strange clay animal. The Silvarado Bird explained it was for making poppy tea. The Brown Pelican called it a Poppykettle.

When the seven Hairy Peruvians saw the Poppykettle they cried, "It's perfect! This is the ship for our great sea voyage!"

But the Brown Pelican grumbled, "It's too heavy to carry back to the beach and besides, it's bad luck to steal anything from the sacred city."

The Silverdo Bird said, "Nonsense, I don't believe such stories and I'm strong enough to carry the Poppykettle, her crew, and even you Brown Pelican."

So it was the Silverado Bird that flew the Poppykettle back to a sandy beach at Callao. Here they set to work to prepare for their voyage.

They made a sail, like those they had seen on the ships of the
Shining Spaniards, and painted a picture of the Silverado Bird on it.
  "This will bring us good luck," they said.
Then they filled the ship with the food they would
need for their voyage.

When they tried the Poppykettle on the water, even with all the sacks of food, she was far too light and they worried she would tip over.

"She's top heavy," someone said.

"We need more weight inside," said another.

"More pot weight," said a third.

The Brown Pelican suggested that they might steal a number of brass or iron keys from the Shining Spaniards. These would just fit neatly into the Poppykettle, and would be a fair exchange for all the gold and silver stolen from the Noble Incas. And so they did.

When they were ready to sail, they found there was no one to tow them out to sea.
They needed to catch the wind that blew only in the realm of the Sea God El Niño.
Suddenly a voice said, "The keys you took came from the jewel boxes of the Shining
Spanish ladies. It's a dull and boring life inside those boxes! It will be exciting to help
with such a voyage and I'm not afraid of the Sea God El Niño."

It was the voice of a fish made of silver.

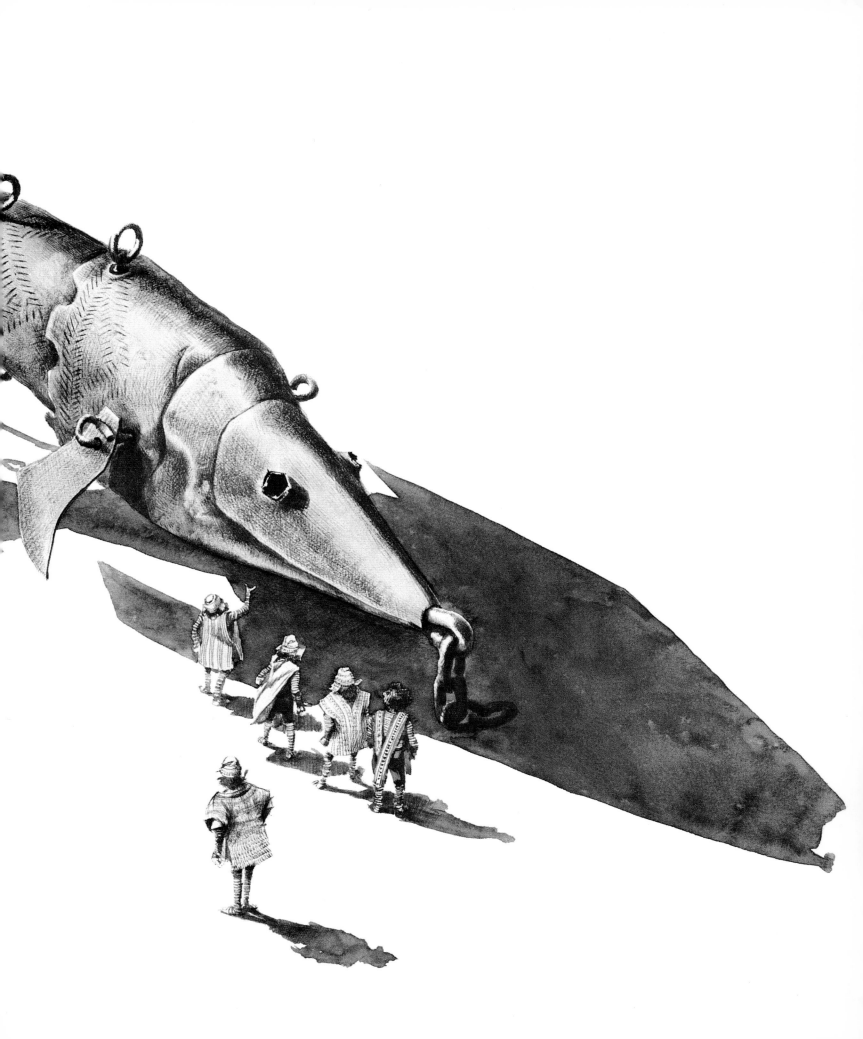

They harnessed the Silver Fish to the Poppykettle and said their goodbyes as he slowly began to tow them out to sea. The Brown Pelican followed for a while but at a safe distance, for he had heard that El Niño liked to have Pelicans as slaves and was nervous that the Hairy Peruvians might meet him.

At the first sign of a breeze they set the Silver Fish free, and sailed unaided for the first time.

"At last our voyage begins!" they cried.

The high peaks of the Andes faded out of sight. The open sea lay all around the Poppykettle, and they kept a careful lookout for signs of the Sea God El Niño.

Fishermen say that El Niño has roamed the ocean waters with his serpent boat and pelican slaves for centuries. He hunts the Great Ocean Fish, but he has never caught it.

This makes him so angry that every few years the heat of his anger warms the seawater. The fish must swim to cooler waters. The birds and fishermen cannot reach them, so they go hungry.

The Hairy Peruvians were lucky. El Niño was not to be seen.

They were spared El Niño, but another adventure was soon upon them. It started with the wind. It blew stronger and stronger, day after day, until it blew the Poppykettle towards some rocky islands.

The spiky iguanas that lived there looked like giant dragons
to the Hairy Peruvians. This could never be their new home.
They were terrified as the wind carried them closer and closer.
The rocks were swarming with the fire-breathing creatures.
The iguanas hissed and snarled as the Poppykettle
came closer. But then an amazing thing happened.
The hot breath of the iguanas actually blew the
Poppykettle away again, to safety. With the wind and
the iguanas the Poppykettle bobbed wildly at sea,
but was finally able to pass the islands.

They sailed on and on across the mighty Pacific Ocean. They saw nothing but the occasional fish. They saw no islands or birds, nothing but water.

The tiny Poppykettle sailed across the rolling sea, bobbing, swaying and dipping. It was a good thing that the Hairy Peruvians were not people who suffered from seasickness.

Days went by.

Then weeks.

Then months.

At last one of the Hairy Peruvians called out, "Reef!"

They all looked where he was pointing and saw an island with palm trees and white sandy beaches. But the surf was breaking on a coral reef which lay between them and the island. The Poppykettle was again in great danger. The surf could easily pick her up and smash her to pieces on the cruel coral rock.

The wind carried them steadily towards the reef, and it seemed that nothing could save them. Suddenly, the head of an old woman rose up beside them from under the water. She had been fishing for food for her family when she saw the danger and lifted the Poppykettle in both hands as if she were going to drink from a precious goblet. She swam around the reef and into the calm lagoon. On reaching the beach she carefully placed the Poppykettle and its startled crew on the gleaming white sand.

The Hairy Peruvians wanted to thank the woman for her kindness, and with difficulty they explained about their search for a new home that was somewhere far beyond the horizon.

The old women finally seemed to understand and showed them a strange thing. It was a grid made of palm strips and cowrie shells all tied together with vines.

"This is our map of the ocean," she said. "The strips show the currents and the direction of the winds. The shells mark where the islands are located."

The tiny hairy sailors studied the map carefully before the old islander carried them out over the reef again, and gently pushed them on their way.

Now they had some idea of what lay ahead. They saw a big sailing canoe, full of big people using long paddles. The old island woman had told the Hairy Peruvians that these boat people had set out from the Land of the Long White Cloud to seek another home among the islands. The Poppykettle was safe because the big paddlers were far too busy to notice the little clay pot bobbing past them in another direction.

Week after week the Poppykettle sailed on towards the west. The weather became colder, and the sky filled with great dark clouds. One morning a violent thunderstorm broke.

Wild gusts of wind churned the ocean into a fury. The whole world around the Poppykettle became so rough that the Hairy Peruvians felt they had reached the end of the earth, and that the thundering waves would wash them over the edge.

One moment they were forced under the water and next they were flying high in the air.

One of the crew lost his grip and was washed overboard. They could do nothing to save him. They were afraid he was lost forever.

The storm raged on for days, nobody knew exactly how many, and then it died away as quickly as it had started. The Poppykettle had suffered great damage. A wide crack was letting in water. The water started covering the keys and the sacks of food as their little boat sank lower in the calm sea. They were sinking fast and there was nothing they could do but wait for their adventure to come to an end.

Then as if from nowhere, a curious dolphin swam up to the sinking broken pot. He had followed the Poppykettle during the storm, more out of curiosity than with the idea of being helpful. He was headed to the waters far to the southwest. But when he saw the damage to the Poppykettle he knew he must help.

"I think I could lift you out of the water with my head," he said. "If you want, I'll take you along with me. You had better figure out some way to hold on."

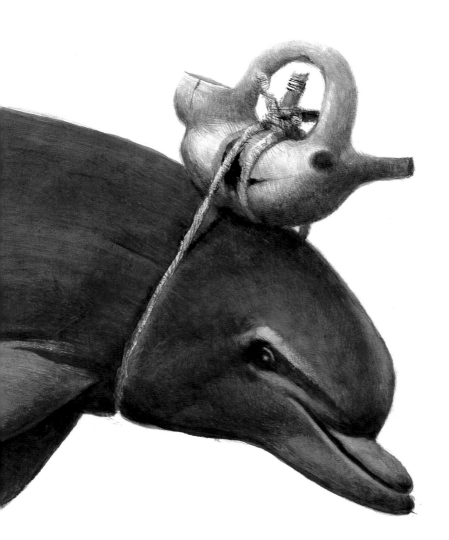

The Hairy Peruvians made a rope out of the remains of their sail. They tied the Poppykettle to the head of the dolphin, and he gently raised them out of the water.

"Hold on tight!" he said. "Here we go!"

He made a couple of test leaps and then they were off. For the Hairy Peruvians it was almost like being in the storm, up in the air one moment and down in the water the next. They seemed safe however, and were definitely going somewhere fast.

After many days the dolphin began to slow down and they approached a long low coastline perhaps as long as Peru, except there were no mountains in the far distance. The dolphin knew where he was going as he made his way into a calm bay.

He didn't stop there, but glided through to another sheltered bay.

"Here you go," he said. "You can hop off now. I have places to go and I can't be seen carrying a clay pot on my head."

He tipped the Poppykettle and its crew onto the beach, said goodbye and swam off with a flip of his tail.

The weary Hairy Peruvians looked around wondering whether this was the new home they had been looking for, or was it just another stop on their long journey.

One thing was for sure: their Poppykettle would never sail again.

The crack had widened during the journey aboard the dolphin. Now it was so big that two keys fell through onto the sand. They looked sadly at their faithful ship, and gathered some sacks of food and other useful items. As they explored this new place they realized that this "Unchosen Land" would be their new home.

That first night on land after four years at sea they set up a camp beside a spring of fresh water. It was a beautiful place really, surrounded by strange trees and grasses. Even the sounds and smells were different. It was not like Peru, but they would make it their home.

Finally, they were home.

Exactly 263 years after the dolphin tipped the Poppykettle onto the beach, two men were digging in the side of a cliff on Corio Bay near Geelong in Victoria, Australia. One of their shovels clinked against metal, and they dug out two ancient brass keys. Nobody could understand why old keys should be buried so deep in the cliff. In that year, 1847, white settlers had only been in Geelong for a short time. The Australian Aborigines never used metal objects like keys.

The Governor of the colony, Charles La Trobe, visited the spot on what is now called Limeburner's Point. He calculated that the keys must have been there for hundreds of years to be buried so deeply. Many people saw the old keys and wrote about them in newspapers. But nobody could explain how they got there.

Could it be that these were the keys which fell out of the Poppykettle? But what happened to the Hairy Peruvians and the remains of their ship? Was their "Unchosen Land" really Australia?

That is another story.

AND NOW...
Today, the school children of Geelong celebrate Poppykettle Day every October. They have been doing so for many, many years.
Few children know, however, exactly why they do this, or even understand how it came to be part of their school life.

The story of the Poppykettle and its crew is a celebration of the imagination. By taking a few facts and wrapping them in a parcel of invention, it helps make reality more interesting.

Maybe that's the reason for the celebration, or maybe for the children it's simply something fun to do.

LA MER

ORIENTA

CAPRI

MADAGASCAR: OV
Sainct Laurens.

madagascar

AVSTRALLE: